The Sleepover Club

Have you been
invited to all these
sleepovers?

1. The Sleepover Club at Frankie's
2. The Sleepover Club at Lyndsey's
3. The Sleepover Club at Felicity's
4. The Sleepover Club at Rosie's
5. The Sleepover Club at Kenny's
6. Starring the Sleepover Club
7. The Sleepover Girls Go Spice
8. The 24 Hour Sleepover Club
9. The Sleepover Club Sleeps Out
10. Happy Birthday, Sleepover Club
11. Sleepover Girls on Horseback
12. Sleepover in Spain
13. Sleepover on Friday 13th
14. Sleepover Girls at Camp
15. Sleepover Girls Go Detective
16. Sleepover Girls Go Designer
17. The Sleepover Club Surfs the Net
18. Sleepover Girls on Screen
19. Sleepover Girls and Friends
20. Sleepover Girls on the Catwalk
21. The Sleepover Club Goes for Goal!

Sleepover Girls
Go Babysitting

by Angie Bates

Collins
An Imprint of HarperCollinsPublishers

The Sleepover Club ® is a
registered trademark of HarperCollins*Publishers* Ltd

First published in Great Britain by Collins in 1999
Collins is an imprint of HarperCollins*Publishers* Ltd
77-85 Fulham Palace Road, Hammersmith,
London, W6 8JB

The HarperCollins website address is
www.**fire**and**water**.com

1 3 5 7 9 8 6 4 2

Text copyright © Angie Bates 1999

Original series characters, plotlines
and settings © Rose Impey 1997

ISBN 0 00675454-6

The author asserts the moral right to
be identified as the author of the work.

Printed and bound in Great Britain by
Caledonian International Book Manufacturing Ltd,
Glasgow G64

Sleepover Kit List

1. Sleeping bag
2. Pillow
3. Pyjamas or a nightdress
4. Slippers
5. Toothbrush, toothpaste, soap etc
6. Towel
7. Teddy
8. A creepy story
9. Food for a midnight feast:
   chocolate, crisps, sweets, biscuits.
   In fact anything you like to eat.
10. Torch
11. Hairbrush
12. Hair things like a bobble or hairband,
    if you need them
13. Clean knickers and socks
14. Change of clothes for the next day
15. Sleepover diary and membership card

CHAPTER ONE

Oh, hiya. No fooling you Sleepover fans, is there! Yes, it's me, Frankie! Look, it's great to meet you here, but please don't tell anyone else you've seen me.

I'm serious. I'm keeping a low profile until this whole thing blows over. Why do you think I sneaked out of the house in dark glasses and this sad saggy old hat?

Lucky for me Grandpa Joe left his fishing hat behind last time he stayed. Yeah, yeah, I know; it's not the coolest head-gear in the world. For one thing, it smells like mouldy mushrooms. But it's brilliant for hiding my hair. Especially with my collar turned up.

I've got masses of the stuff. Hair, I mean. Auntie Joan says I could stuff a mattress with it. I figured my hair was the real Frankie giveaway. Apart from my lanky legs, that is. But there's nothing I can do about them, unless I disguise myself as a mermaid!

Anyway, I'm glad it was you, not the M&Ms who spotted me. Remember them? They're sworn enemies of the Sleepover Club. Their real names are Emma Hughes and Emily Berryman. We call them the M&Ms for short. Neat, eh?

You see, on our last sleepover, quite by accident, we did something the M&Ms will NEVER forgive us for. And take it from me, they won't give up till they've paid us back. Those girls are so spiteful it's *unreal*.

Would you mind looking out for them, while I pull Grandpa's hat down a teensy bit further? Don't worry, they're dead easy to recognise. Look out for two sinister figures without shadows. Just kidding! No, you nutcase, I'm not scared! But I don't need any extra hassle. I'm still totally stressed out from our last sleepover.

OK, let's just see if you remember all the Sleepover members. There's a whole bunch of us: Laura McKenzie, otherwise known as Kenny. She's been my best friend for ever. Then Fliss. (Her full name is Felicity Sidebotham, poor thing.) Lyndsey Collins – we call her Lyndz. And Rosie Cartwright; Rosie hasn't lived in Cuddington very long.

And then there's me! Francesca Theresa Thomas, Frankie for short. But you guessed that by yourself, didn't you? I'll have to get better at disguises, if I'm going to be a world-famous actress! It was my nail varnish that gave me away, right?

I'm crazy about silver. It's the coolest colour in the universe. I'd paint my whole room silver if my parents would let me. Up till now they won't even let me have silver curtains! And now Mum's expecting a new baby, I can probably kiss goodbye to that space-age bedroom I've been hankering for. My parents are too busy buying cute little vests and booties.

Actually I'm over the moon about the baby. Being a lonely only is *so-o* bo-ring. But Mum's pregnancy doesn't mean I'm letting them off the hook. I don't want them to think I've lost my touch! Besides, I think a totally silver room would be excellent, don't you? Not as good as sleeping in a real space station, but still pretty cool. I could even camouflage my boring old bed to look like a space pod or something. Mind you, I'm not sure the other Sleepover members would approve. Especially Fliss. Her bedroom furniture looks exactly like that shiny stuff in department stores. It's dead girly – like a Barbie catalogue. And her room's so tidy, it's scary!

Still, what can you expect from a Virgo? I'm an Aries, if you didn't know. A natural born leader. Act first and think afterwards, that's me.

Where was I? Oh yeah. I was explaining why I'm creeping round the village wearing this gruesome disguise.

Have you noticed how the things which seem totally mega-brilliant at the time, are the exact same things which make your parents go ballistic when they find out? Life's so-o-o unfair.

Look, pop over to Rosie's with me and I'll tell you all the really *juicy* details of our sleepover as we go. (Private joke!) I could do with the company. Don't tell the others, but I've got butterflies in my tummy.

You see, I promised Rosie I'd tell Mr and Mrs Quormby what really happened, and I can't let her down, can I? I'm going to be someone's big sister in two months. I've got to practise being dead grown-up and sensible before he or she arrives.

Didn't I explain about the Quormbys? They're Rosie's new neighbours. They've got this really cool baby called Morgan. Mr Quormby's the grim silent type. Mrs Quormby's OK, but she's such a fusspot! Can you believe she'd never ever left her precious little Morgan with anyone before? Not even for five minutes!

Until last Friday that is...

No one believes us, but the whole thing started out as an incredibly kind deed. Two kind deeds, if you're counting.

It began when Rosie's big sister Tiff and her boyfriend Spud had a quarrel. We could tell Rosie was upset the minute she walked into the classroom. When Rosie's upset, everyone knows about it. Of course, she won't actually tell you what's wrong for hours. Her star sign's Cancer. Sensitive but secretive, that's Rosie. She's such hard work sometimes.

It took us nearly all lunchtime to drag it out of her. Then instead of just telling us like a normal person, she turned on the waterworks. And once she gets started, that girl could cry for England.

"Tiff and Spud broke up," she choked. "I heard her sobbing through the wall. It was awful."

"Poor Tiffany," said Fliss, with that mushy look she gets if anyone even mentions boyfriends.

Tiff is Rosie's big sister. She's fifteen.

Personally, I don't think she's that special. I mean, the way Rosie goes on you'd think she's some kind of superstar. But when I pictured little Miss Perfect crying in the dark over some stoopid boy, I felt a bit upset myself. Even though I don't like her. Weird, eh?

"What about Adam?" asked Lyndz. "He really likes Spud, doesn't he?" Lyndz has a soft spot for Adam, since he helped us save her riding school that time.

Rosie nodded miserably. "They talk about computers for hours."

I yawned. Computers are cool, but talking about them is incredibly sad. I suppose it's different for Adam, though. He's got cerebral palsy and his computer helps him speak and everything.

"So of course Dad's invited Adam to stay for the weekend," Rosie moaned.

Rosie and Adam are great mates. But that doesn't stop her getting all churned up about how their dad spends more time with her brother than he does with her. She's got this huge chip about how everyone in her family leaves her out. She's always on about it, so now I switch off as soon as she starts.

I tuned back in just as Rosie said, "So we can't have the sleepover at my house after all. Mum says it's not fair to Tiff."

Now, nothing and no one interrupts Sleepover business, OK? Especially not Tiffany Cartwright's love life. I did some quick thinking.

"Why don't you tell us exactly what happened, Rosie," I said cunningly. "Tell us everything. I mean, what did they fight about?"

Kenny saw how my mind was working.

"Yeah, Rosie," she grinned. "We need inside info."

Rosie blinked with surprise. We mostly shut her up when she goes on about her family!

"It's obvious Tiff and Spud are dotty about each other," I explained. "They just need a teensy bit of help. Then they'll snap back together like... like... fridge magnets!"

Lyndz, Kenny and Fliss cracked up. Even Rosie gave a feeble grin.

I beamed. Crisis over. We'd get those love-birds back together, no problem. Easy peasy lemon squeezy. And our sleepover could go ahead like we planned. YIPPEE!

CHAPTER TWO

Wait a tick. I'm stopping the story right here. Sto-op!!!

I'm not telling you another thing until you understand exactly why we hate the M&Ms so much. Because right now, you think we're mean about them for no reason, don't you? Admit it!

It's not just because they smarm up to the teachers all the time, you know. And get top marks in everything. Even though that's incredibly icky of them. No, we hate them because they're spiteful little toads who try to ruin everything for us. Don't believe me? Okay, I'll prove it to you!

Remember how I told you about Rosie blurting out that dead private stuff about Spud and Tiffany?

Can you believe those creepy girls were actually spying on us the whole time, soaking up every word?

Understand why we hate them now? Coo-ell! Then I'll tell you the rest.

It's really true about them spying. When we went into our classroom, Emma Hughes started dabbing her eyes, pretending to cry. "Oh Emily, isn't it too sad about Tiffany and Spud?"

"Oh yes, Emma," sniffled Emily. "I haven't cried so much since my Gran's budgie fell off its perch."

"Tiffany's so-o-o beautiful," sighed Emma.

"And darling Spud is so-o-o hunky. Not!"

They made being-sick noises.

I thought Rosie was going to bop Emma one. She hasn't had much practice dealing with the M&Ms and it shows. But don't worry!

17

Good ole Kenny was already on the case.

"Frankie," she said in a chatty voice, "do you think those sad little androids will ever get, you know, a life?"

Honestly, I nearly kissed her. "I wish, Kenny," I sighed. "They must be so-o-o bored."

"Yeah," Lyndz joined in. "Why else would they hang around us all the time, earwigging people's private conversations?"

Emma Hughes' mouth opened like a goldfish, but before she got a word out, Fliss started up.

"I'm sorry for them, aren't you?" she said in a saintly voice. "They must feel really empty inside." She put on a tragic face, but we knew she was dying to laugh. We all were.

Rosie finally caught on. "Do you think those poor girls secretly admire us?" she asked, all wide-eyed.

"Could be," Kenny agreed. "They'll be copying us next. Having sad little sleepovers with Alana Banana."

You should have seen the M&Ms squirm! They kept making strangled noises but every time they tried to get a word in, one of us got in first. It was brilliant! But it got even better.

"Can't you picture them in their frilly nighties?" I said.

"Drinking up their nice hot malted milk," said Lyndz.

I did my Alana-the-android imitation. "Goodness me, Emma and Emily. Who could have dreamed that sleeping over would be this much fun. Is it nearly time for our exciting midnight feast yet?"

"It certainly is, Alana Banana. But do be careful not to get any nasty crumbs in Mummy's sheets," said Kenny, taking off Emma's snooty voice.

I wish you'd seen their prune faces! They were as sick as parrots.

"We know how to have fun, thanks very much," shrieked Emma Hughes.

Emily Berryman tossed her hair. "Yeah," she said. "We don't need you losers to show us, do we, Alana?"

"No way," echoed Alana, their creepy slave.

And honestly she sounded exactly like a sad little robot. That did it. We laughed till we cried.

Our teacher, Miss Weaver, came in just then. "You seem to be having fun," she said cheerfully. She couldn't understand why me, Kenny and the others fell about.

Kenny poked me in the back. "Was that a result, or was that a result?" she hissed.

"Yeah, one–nil to us," I hissed back. "And it's not over yet!"

It wasn't. Not nearly. I was more determined than ever to get Spud and Tiff back together. I mean, to start with I'd only wanted to save our sleepover. But now I wanted to save Spud and Tiff too. That would show those sneery little witches!

I kept picturing it, like a scene from a soap. Tiff all pink and happy. And poor old Spud staring at his boots, telling her how sorry he was. I didn't know how we were going to make this mushy scene come true, mind you. But each time I replayed it in my mind, the more real it seemed. Then all at once I'd got it.

A totally brilliant plan!!

I know what you're thinking! Frankie Thomas, playing Cupid. This is all a bad dream, right? Yeah, yeah. I don't understand it either. But it's not true what people say about only children. We aren't all selfish little so-and-sos, you know. Besides, I'm not an only any more. I'm going to be a big sister like Tiff. Who knows, I might need a favour myself one day!

Anyway, when it was afternoon break, we streaked straight into the playground and grabbed our favourite corner. You've got to be quick off the mark if you want any privacy at our school. Unless you like being tripped up by sad little kids droning "Five little speckled frogs"!

Lyndz split her packet of Skittles with us. Then I made Rosie run through Spud and Tiff's quarrel again to make sure she hadn't left out something important. Don't give me that look. I'm NOT a bossy boots, OK. But someone has to get the show on the road, and it's usually me.

"It was Tiff and Spud's anniversary,"

explained Rosie. "They've been going out a whole year. So Spud was meant to be taking Tiff to the multiplex to see that James Bond film."

"Coo-ell," said Lyndz. "My brother says James Bond's new girlfriend is wicked."

"Yeah, she does mega stunts on a motorbike," said Kenny.

"I saw her on telly," sighed Fliss. "She's got a figure to die for."

Some days I feel like I'm the only girl in the Sleepover Club with brain cells. I took a big breath. "BUT LOVER BOY FORGOT TO TURN UP, OK!" I bellowed, to get their attention.

Kenny rubbed her ears. "Keep your hair on, Spaceman."

"Sorry Rosie," said Lyndz.

"Spud did worse than just forget," Rosie went on. "He actually went off to football practice with his mates."

"Duh," said Lyndz. "What a nerd."

"I don't see what's nerdy about that," said Kenny. For reasons none of us understand, football is totally sacred to Kenny. And anyone who dares to criticise her favourite team, Leicester City, is in big trouble.

"I think it's awful," said Fliss dramatically. "It shows some stupid game is more important to Spud than his feelings for Tiffany." Sometimes Fliss talks like a problem page.

Kenny had an evil glint in her eye. "Football's not stupid."

"Let Rosie finish, you wallies. The bell's going any minute."

So Rosie told us how her sister kept ringing the cinema to see when the next showing was. Tiffany thought she'd got the times wrong at first. Then she finally realised Spud wasn't coming. But she didn't make a big fuss or anything. Just shut herself in her room and finished her homework. See what I mean? There's something unnatural about that girl.

Of course, next day old Spud breezes round, as if nothing's happened. When he let slip where he'd been, Tiff totally flipped. Being a Cartwright, she didn't explain why she was upset, of course. Just did what we call her Ice Queen routine and sent Spud packing.

"Now he thinks she hates him," Rosie said, her lip trembling.

"Cheer up," I said. "Those two are going to live happily ever after if it kills us!"

For a minute Rosie looked exactly like my little dog Pepsi, when she thinks you're taking her for a walk; all hopeful, with her head on one side. "Do you really think so, Frankie?" she quavered.

"I know so," I beamed. "I've got a plan."

And if I say so myself, when the others heard it, they were pretty impressed.

"Hey," said Kenny, as we went back into school. "Anyone notice the M&Ms snooping round that time?"

"Not unless they were disguised as dustbins," giggled Fliss.

We finally spotted them in a huddle with Alana and Regina Hill. The M&Ms, I mean, not the dustbins! Alana made this big thing of shutting her sad little teen magazine and putting it away, to stop us seeing who they were drooling over. But I'd already clocked it. Probably because Juice is the only pop singer I actually know personally.

I'm not swanking. It's the truth!

He wasn't a singer when I knew him, though. Just this weird kid called Julian Whately who lived next door to a friend of Mum's. Then he dyed his hair, changed his name, and became this, like, big superstar. And if you want my honest opinion, he's still a dork. It's a total mystery to me why so many girls go wild about him For some reason, the M&Ms had got it bad for Juice. I heard them whispering about him all afternoon. But I couldn't care less what they were cooking up. I didn't have time. I was working out what we were going to say to Spud after school.

CHAPTER THREE

I don't know about you, but if I was going out with a boy, I'd personally prefer one with a sensible name. I mean, what kind of name is SPUD? Sounds like a labrador with gruesome breath! Also, you'd think someone called Spud would look tough, wouldn't you? You know, with a serious tattoo or a stubbly haircut. But Tiff's Spud's got this fluffy yellow hair. Kenny says he looks like an ugly little duckling!

Anyway, we hit the Happy Shopper at 3.30pm on the dot. Both Tiff and Spud work there after school, which at this moment they were probably REALLY regretting.

Luckily for us, Spud was stacking tins of sweetcorn miles from the checkout. Tiffany works on the till, you see. If she rumbled what we were up to, it would ruin everything.

As we went through the door, Kenny muttered into her collar, "Operation Cupid, Phase One." So then Fliss started up with the theme tune from *Mission Impossible*. "Dum dum der der dum dum..." This was the first time in the history of the Sleepover Club Fliss has done anything so mad! So of course we rushed straight out again in hysterics.

"Don't," gasped Lyndz. "Suppose I get my hiccups?"

I pulled myself together. "We'll just strangle you." Lyndz is famous for hiccups. She gets them at the worst times. And before you offer me your favourite family hiccup cure, believe me, that girl's tried them ALL!

Just then we spotted Tiff through the window, checking through a massive bag of frozen peas.

"She looks terrible," said Lyndz.

Kenny nudged me. "Spud doesn't look too great either."

"He keeps giving Tiff these sad little looks," breathed Fliss. "He really loves her." Fliss is truly mushy.

"Come on," I said firmly. "Operation Cupid is going for it this time."

In we went. We'd agreed that Rosie was dealing with Spud. Luckily she can wind him round her finger. As the rest of us slid past, we heard her say sweetly, "Hiya Spud."

Actually I'm beginning to think she has hidden depths. In fact I'm dead jealous. You see, my original plan was for Rosie to pretend she'd twisted her ankle. But Kenny sensibly pointed out that Rosie's mum would then naturally rush her off to Leicester Royal Infirmary for X-rays. "And by the time she's spent three hours in casualty and found out Rosie's shamming, she's going to be in a real razz," she said.

Kenny's big on anything medical. She's going to be a doctor like her dad. She was right, too. If Rosie's mum suspected a set-up, we'd never get our sleepover, not to mention the fact that Rosie would be in doom for ever!

Then Rosie came up with a wicked variation on my plan. I wasn't too sure she'd bring it off. I don't want to boast, but I'm the actress, right? Yeah, yeah, don't get your undies in a twist. I'll get to the point, if you give me a chance.

Where was I? Yeah, the Happy Shopper. Well, the rest of us were acting all innocent, filling our basket with Special Offer snowballs (snowballs are the Sleepover Club's new obsession. They're dee-licious white squidgy things coated in coconut, if you don't know) when Spud came skidding round the corner.

"Tiff, Tiff!" he croaked. "Rosie's fainted."

That boy's wasted as a footballer. He should go on stage!

Tiff jumped up and went sprinting down the aisles. We flocked after her like anxious little lambs.

Rosie was stretched out on the floor with her eyes closed. When Fliss saw her, she gave a huge gulp as if she felt faint too. Fainting's catching, I don't know why.

"Are you sure she's not pretending?" Tiff whispered. She patted her sister's cheek. "Rosie?" she said. Rosie's eyelids fluttered and she gave a moan.

"Tiff?" she croaked. "What happened? Where am I?" Rosie opened her eyes and looked round.

Was that an Oscar-winning faint or what!

"Tiff, I just remembered," I said. "Someone pinched Rosie's lunch at school."

"Yeah, poor Rosie. She only had a couple of Skittles, didn't she Lyndz?" Kenny said, keeping a wickedly straight face.

Lyndz just nodded. "Mmm," she mumbled, terrified her hiccups would start up and wreck everything.

"Her blood sugar probably dropped to zero," Kenny added.

"It's OK, Rosie," said Tiff. "You fainted, that's all."

"She's all right now, aren't you, Rosie?" I said.

Rosie sat up. "I'm fine," she said feebly. "I just need to go home and eat something. Tiff, will you take me? I feel a bit wobbly."

Didn't we all!

"I'll take you," said Spud quickly. "Tiffany can't leave the till, can you?"

She blushed and shook her head. And then and there, Spud picked Rosie up in his arms and strode out with her. Well, he did stagger a teensy bit, but it was still totally and utterly brilliant.

Tiff stared after him, looking almost as woozy as Rosie.

"Spud is such a star," sighed Kenny. "He seemed really upset about something though, didn't you think, Frankie?"

"Yeah, sort of haunted." I jumped as if I'd forgotten Tiff was there. "Ooh, sorry, Tiffany. Nearly forgot to pay for these," I said.

Fliss gazed mistily through the window, still acting her socks off. "Poor Spud," she said. "What in the world could be making him so-o-o sad?"

I deliberately didn't look at Tiff but I heard

her give a little gasp of sorrow, so I just knew we'd got a result!

I couldn't wait to ring Rosie and find out if our plan was working. But in the end I had to wait after all.

That night the Cartwrights' phone was engaged for hours. Mum kept telling me to go to bed, but I insisted I had to know if Rosie was OK. "Or what kind of friend would I be?" I demanded.

"Hmm," said Mum, looking dead suspicious. I had to distract her by admiring her latest Mothercare buys. Actually, I think being pregnant is sending Mum slightly off her head. I'm sure she's buying doll's clothes by mistake. There's no way a real person could fit into those dinky little things!

Finally I got through to Rosie. "Feeling better, poor little Rosie-Posie?" I giggled. "Or did Spud drop you on your head?"

"Don't make me laugh," whispered Rosie. "I can't talk now."

"Just tell me the important bit. Did we get a result? Yes or no will do!"

"Yes," Rosie breathed in my ear.

"YES!" I punched the air.

"Rosie's feeling better now, I presume," Mum called in that sarky tone grown-ups use when they think they see right through you.

"So is our sleepover safe or not, Rosie?" I hissed.

"It's safe," Rosie hissed back. "But there's... erm... a complication."

"Another one?" I yelped. "Like what?"

"I'll explain tomorrow," she said. "Gotta go. I've got to tidy my room for our sleepover."

Rosie and her mum are paranoid about visitors. Even us, Rosie's very best friends. When they first moved here, Rosie's dad did all this radical DIY – hacked off plaster and generally bashed the place about. Then he walked out for ever, leaving them in a house that looks like a bomb site. We fixed up Rosie's bedroom a while back, but the rest of the house is still a mess. Her Dad says he's going to come and help do things up, but he never gets round to it.

I put down the phone feeling mega fed up. I was going to have to wait all night to find out what Rosie was on about. Don't you just hate that!!

CHAPTER FOUR

I couldn't believe it. First Rosie makes me wait all night, then next day she didn't even show up!

"I bet she's really ill now," said Fliss. "I knew she shouldn't have faked that faint. This sleepover's totally doomed." Fliss is dead superstitious.

"Double doomed," grumbled Kenny. Kenny isn't superstitious at all. She was just in a really bad mood!

To our relief Rosie appeared after lunch. "Mum only dragged me to the doctor's," she said, pulling a face.

Her mum wanted to make sure Rosie didn't have some fatal fainting disease. The doctor said Rosie was as fit as a frog, which she thought was really rude. "I hate Doctor Mackie," moaned Rosie. "He treats me as if I was five. And I hate that gruesome shoehorn he uses to see your tonsils. Yuk!"

Kenny's eyes gleamed. "They're called tongue depressors," she said. "I can't wait to use one."

"So what's this new problem, Rosie?" By this time I was beginning to think Rosie's sleepover was under a curse too!

Rosie took a deep breath. "Mum's been invited to the Harrisons. It's some big welcome party for the Quormbys. They're the ones with the baby, remember?"

"Tiff will be home though, won't she?" asked Fliss.

"Kind of," said Rosie uncomfortably.

"You're so weird, Rosie," giggled Lyndz. "How can someone be 'kind of' home? She's not invisible, like the Invisible Man, is she?"

"I meant she'll be kind of busy," explained Rosie. "With the baby. Usually the Quormbys take Morgan with them when they go out. But Mr Quormby thinks it's time they used a babysitter. So Mum volunteered Tiff. That way, if anything goes wrong, they'll only be over the road."

"You said this sleepover was safe," I groaned. "I wish your mum would make up her mind."

"It is! She did!" said poor Rosie. "Only she thought our sleepover was off until last night, didn't she? But now Tiff's got back with Spud, she told Mum the sleepover's cool with her."

Honestly you'd think Tiffany was the Princess of Cuddington, the way Rosie goes on.

"But why isn't Tiff babysitting for Morgan over at the Quormbys?" said Lyndz, puzzled.

"Well, that was the original plan. But Mum rang the Quormbys to explain about our sleepover. So now they're bringing Morgan to our place. Mum swears the baby is totally no trouble. So you can all still come." Rosie's eyes were huge with worry. "It's just that there's going to be this little baby there. Is that OK? Or do you all really hate me?"

For some reason Rosie thinks we'll go off her if she ever lets the Sleepover Club down, like once !

"It's OK with me," said Kenny looking round. "What about you lot?"

"I lurve little babies," said Fliss.

"What about Frankie?" asked Rosie.

"It's cool," I said. "I need all the big-sister practice I can get."

"Lyndz?"

"No problem. Sounds just like home," she said cheerfully. Lyndz has got four brothers, including a baby brother, Spike.

Rosie beamed with relief. "Thanks, guys! I was really—"

But then this sickly sweet singing started up, drowning her out.

You know when people try to sound like pop singers, but they can't actually sing a note? And they still think they're totally the bees' knees?

Yes, strange but true! It was the Gruesome Twosome, Emma and Emily, with their creepy backing singer Alana Banana, murdering Juice's latest hit, *Forever Love.*

"Poor ole Juice," giggled Lyndz. "Imagine being fancied by the M&Ms!"

"Imagine fancying Juice," I said. "He needs a babysitter if you ask me. He's got a real baby face."

"That's why he wears those huge trousers," spluttered Kenny. "To make room for his nappy."

I fell about. But Fliss went all huffy.

"Juice is sweet. And *Forever Love* is a brilliant song."

"It's OK so long as you don't have to clock his nappy while he's singing."

I got the giggles again. We all did. Well, except Fliss.

"I don't know why you're laughing," she said stiffly. "It's not that funny."

That set Lyndz off again. "Yes it is!" she spluttered. "Hic! Oh, no!" she wailed.

"Not again," we groaned. We marched

Lyndz off to the toilets and experimented with dropping her own door key down her neck a few times. But that just made her need to go to the loo. Then we all had to go – you know how it is.

But while we were in there, we discovered why the M&Ms were killing Juice's song. We were wondering! (Probably you were too?)

Remember Kenny's crack about the M&Ms having their own sad little sleepovers? Well, like Gran says, "Many a true word spoken in jest."

You've guessed, haven't you? Don't laugh! This is deadly serious. Those little clones were planning the first M&M sleepover in history. Is that gruesome or what? We heard Alana tell Regina when we were in the loos.

Naturally the M&Ms don't have a clue what normal kids do at sleepovers. So they were devoting the night to their new heartthrob. Playing Juice songs and sighing over stupid pop magazines, you know – the kind that describe pop stars' favourite colours and what jelly they like. Gosh, bet you wish you'd been invited! (NOT!!)

Alana was trying to persuade Regina to sleep over with them. "We really want you to," she whined.

"I bet they do," Lyndz muttered, from the next loo. "Regina's the only one who sings in tune."

"Don't go over to the dark side, Regina," chanted a spooky voice from one of the toilets. It was Kenny. She's such a laugh. But what she said was true too. Regina's new to our school. And we still can't work out if she's in with the M&Ms or not. Like Gran says, she's an unknown quantity.

When we came out and were washing our hands, Alana gave Kenny a spiteful look. "You girls are such babies," she spat.

"You're the ones who fancy a singer in a nappy," I said, and we sailed past with our noses in the air.

I'm sorry to say, the rest of the day was one big yawn. Unless you lurve long division. So hold on tight, OK, while I fast-forward us to the good bit. The part where I finally went home with Rosie.

Rosie's mum had told my mum I could go straight from school. I think Mum was glad of the rest actually. She gets really tired now.

Rosie's house is so brilliant, even though it is a bit of a wreck. When we got there it was full of the most de-licious baking smell.

"Chocolate cake," I thought. "Yummee!"

Tiff makes wicked cakes. She does ace popcorn too, if you get her in a good mood.

Rosie's mum had just got home from college and she had to belt round organising Adam. He was still going to stay with his dad, even though Tiff had cheered up again. The taxi came just as we finished singing *Forever Love* to him. We'd sung it twice. The first time just to take off the M&Ms. But Adam enjoyed it so much, we sang it again. Before he went, Adam typed us a message on his computer. It said, "Juice is a cool dude!"

"You ARE kidding!" I said. I think he was. You can never tell with Adam. He has a truly weird sense of humour!

CHAPTER FIVE

The minute the taxi disappeared, Rosie's mum had to rush around getting ready for the party. Tiff was in charge of tea. Want to know what we had? We had oven chips, crinkly ones, and some excellent chilli burgers that Rosie's mum had bought for me specially.

I was expecting Tiff to break out the chocolate cake for afters. I was so-o-o fed up when it turned out to be Spud's special anniversary cake.

"A whole cake for Spud? Can't we have a tiny slice?" I moaned to Rosie.

Tiff heard me. "No way," she said.

"It's not personal, Frankie. She wouldn't let me even look at it," said Rosie.

So we had ice cream instead. They only had vanilla, but Her Royal Tiffiness said we could invent our own toppings if we wanted. So we really went for it! Heh heh heh!

This is what we put in them: chopped up Dime bar, rainbow drops (another Sleepover obsession!), walnuts, banana, left-over pineapple chunks. Ooh! And glace cherries. Eat your heart out, Ben and Jerry!

By the time we'd finished, I was truly stuffed. We all helped wash up, then Tiffany went off to her room, humming *Forever Love*. It turns out she's a Juice fan too!

"Quick! Come and see my sister's new dress," said Rosie and she dragged me into the living room. I wasn't in the mood to admire anything of Tiffany's after that cake stunt, to be honest. But it was heavenly. It was even the right colour – silver!

"She saved up for it for ages," explained Rosie.

"It's gorgeous," I whispered. I don't know why we were whispering. I mean, it was only a dress – not, like, church!

"Tiff wanted to take it back to the shop, after the quarrel," Rosie wittered on. "Now she's wearing it to the school dance. She looks totally amazing in it."

Yawn yawn yawn. I hate Rosie's Tiffany-worshipping moods. To distract her, I said she should ask Tiff to make some popcorn. "She owes us!" I said.

"Sssh!" hissed Rosie. "She'd go ballistic if she knew I faked that faint!"

"I only asked," I snapped. Honestly, what is the point of a good deed if you can't get a bowl of popcorn out of it?

Luckily, the others turned up then.

"Ooh, yummy! Tiff's made one of her cakes," said Lyndz.

"Forget it," I said. "It's for boring old Spud."

We carried the sleepover gear upstairs. Kenny immediately checked out the wall on the landing for interesting new graffiti. That's one great thing about the Cartwrights' house. Rosie's allowed to write on the undecorated walls, until they've all been painted!

Kenny chewed her pen. Finally she wrote 'ROSIE LOVES JUICE'. Fliss grabbed the pen, drew a swirly heart round Kenny's graffiti and wrote 'TRUE!'

"I do love Juice," beamed Rosie. "Orange juice, apple juice, lime juice, lemon juice, pineapple juice, mango ju..."

I threw my teddy at her. "Knock it off, or we'll juice you, OK?"

Lyndz took something out of her bag. "Look what I've brought."

"Wow!" I said. "A plastic thing with a hole in. Can I have one?"

"It's a bubble sword, you moron," Lyndz explained. "Tom got it at a fair. The proper stuff ran out after half a minute, but we refilled it with Fairy Liquid and it's still brilliant."

It was. First you dip the sword in the part with the bubble stuff in, the scabbard thing. Then you wave the sword and zillions of HUGE bubbles stream out. If there's a fair near you, make your parents take you immediately and DEMAND a bubble sword. They're ace!

We ran around filling the house with bubbles, screaming our heads off.

"I love staying at your place, Rosie," I yelled.

Rosie went bright red. "Thanks, Frankie."

Kenny blew a massive bubble. "It's bigger than my head!" she shrieked.

"It's not bigger than Juice's," I shouted.

"You're so mean," giggled Fliss.

The door bell went.

"Can you get it?" called Rosie's mum in a muffled voice. "I'm still putting my dress on."

Rosie raced for the door, but bossy ole Princess Tiffany beat her to it. It was Mrs Quormby, with the baby.

"Aaah," said everyone. Morgan has to be the most gorgeous baby on the planet. (Until ours arrives, of course.) Mr Quormby followed with the travel cot.

"Hello, girls," he said. But I could tell he only spoke to us because we were in the hall admiring his baby and he couldn't avoid us.

After that, he hung around looking dead bored, while Mrs Quormby made Tiffany stick hundreds of emergency phone numbers on the fridge. She even gave Tiff the number of her mobile, in case the Harrisons' phone was out of order!!! The Quormbys used to live in London, so I suppose Cuddington is practically the Third World to them.

Finally she gave Tiffany this bag bulging with spare clothes, nappies, bottles, toys and stuff. "Just a precaution. Morgan's a very good baby really. She always sleeps right through."

Mr Quormby carried the cot into the living room. Rosie's mum came downstairs while Mrs Quormby was tucking Morgan up for the night. She looked so-o glamorous – Rosie's mum, I mean. And really shy. I don't think she'd been out for ages, except for college.

"Ready, everyone?" she said. "Don't worry. Tiff is totally trustworthy."

"Come ON, Lyn," moaned Mr Quormby, like a little kid. "We'll be late for the party."

I don't know why he was in such a rush. He didn't seem like a party animal to me. But Mrs Quormby glanced back nervously and I realised I was still clutching the bubble sword.

"It's just for bubbles," I called hastily. "Not whacking people."

As soon as they'd gone, we went to look at the baby. It was still wide awake, staring round the room with a slightly surprised expression.

"Aaaah," we said again. The baby gave a happy wriggle, as if we were the coolest thing it had seen for ages.

"Tiff," said Rosie. "If we watch Morgan, will you make us some popcorn?"

"Well, I suppose I—" Tiff began.

Then the phone rang. Rosie answered it.

"It's for you, Tiff," she said. "Spud says if he's not allowed to come round tonight, can he talk to you for a bit."

"Ooooh," we giggled. Tiff went pink.

"Shall I tell him you can't, because you're making our popcorn?" asked Rosie daringly.

"I'll talk as long as I want, thanks," snapped Tiff. "I'll take it upstairs." She sprinted off.

Rosie was still holding the receiver. "Oh, hiya Spud," we heard Tiff say.

We crowded round the phone, earwigging like mad. Unfortunately Rosie lost her balance and clunked the phone on the wall.

"Put it DOWN!" Tiff yelled downstairs. "Can't I have any PRIVACY?"

We went back to the living room. Morgan was chatting away in there. Just like a baby Member of Parliament making a speech!

"Aren't you sleepy?" said Fliss, stroking Morgan's cheek.

"Do you think that's like, a real language?" said Kenny. "I mean, can other babies understand it?"

"Who cares!" I said. "Let's cuddle it before Tiff gets back."

"She didn't say we could," said Rosie, looking doubtful.

"She didn't say we couldn't either," Kenny grinned.

I lifted the baby out of its cot. It smelled of

very clean towelling. "Hey, you're heavy, Morgan," I said.

The baby broke into a huge amazed smile.

"Clever thing. It knows its name!" said Fliss. "Hello, Morgan," she cooed.

"Hello, Morgan," said the others.

Each time we said its name, the baby beamed from ear to ear. So we kept saying it, till Lyndz made us stop. "You'll make its little face ache. And it's got such an adorable little face. Yes, you have!"

(Have you noticed how everyone totally loses their marbles the moment they set eyes on a baby? Why is that?)

"Hope it doesn't grow up like Mr Quormby," I said darkly.

"Look at its darling clothes," whispered Rosie.

"They're OshKosh B'Gosh," said Fliss.

"Osh kosh who?" scowled Kenny.

"They make really cool clothes for babies," Fliss explained.

"Let me hold it, Frankie," pleaded Rosie.

"But it likes me."

"Don't be mean. You'll have your own baby soon."

"Yeah," said Kenny. "We all want a go."

But as I handed the baby to Rosie, its expression changed. It didn't look unhappy. Just thoughtful. Then it started making really PRIVATE sounds.

"Uh-oh," said Lyndz. "Put it down, quick."

"Why, what's happening?" asked Rosie nervously.

Kenny turned pale. "Can anyone smell a terrible pong?"

"Oh per-leaze." I rushed to the phone and picked it up. Tiff was still gabbing to Spud on the other end. "Tiff," I panted. "Get down here! It's serious babysitter business. We're running out of oxygen fast."

"Get OFF the phone, Frankie. I'll come down in a MINUTE," barked Tiffany. But she stayed exactly where she was, flirting. Totally trustworthy, eh? Yeah, right!

Look, I'm sorry. I know it's rude to talk about, you know, poo. But don't go, or you'll miss the best bit. Because it wasn't Tiff

who came to our rescue. You'll never guess
who did!

Get ready to be amazed!

CHAPTER SIX

You know that whingeing babies do? Not really crying – more like someone sawing metal? That's the noise Morgan was making.

Kenny stuck her fingers in her ears. "Tell Tiff to make it stop!"

Rosie shook her head. "She won't come till she's ready. Tiff's dead stubborn."

"Great," said Lyndz.

"The poor thing just needs changing," said Fliss.

"Duh," I said. "Like we didn't know! Go on, Lyndz. You do it."

"Uh-uh," said Lyndz. "Poo is strictly for grown-ups."

"Kenny?" I said hopefully.

She swallowed hard. "Sorry," she said. "I lurve blood and gore, but I don't much go for you-know-what."

I sighed. "Then I volunteer Rosie, OK? It's her house."

"Hear that, Rosie?" said Lyndz. "You're Tiff's stunt double."

"Go girl, go girl," we chanted.

"All right," said Rosie unhappily. She dashed out of the room and we heard her rooting in cupboards.

When she came back, we fell about. Rosie is totally weird. I mean, I don't blame her for sticking a peg on her nose. I can even see why she put on big rubber gloves. But swimming goggles!!!

"Don't forget the baby wipes," said Fliss.

Rosie didn't move, so I fetched them.

"Now you need the baby," said Fliss encouragingly.

Rosie started towards the cot, like someone

in a ve-ry slow action replay.

"Durn durn DURN – nappy disposal squad moving in," I whispered.

"Watch out, Rosie. It might explode," Kenny giggled.

"It already DID," said Lyndz, pinching her nose.

The minute the baby saw Rosie, it stopped crying, as if someone had switched it off at the mains. Then its mouth turned down, like a cartoon baby, and it sucked in a HUGE breath.

"Yikes, it's going to scream!" warned Lyndz.

It did. It screamed itself sky-blue purple.

"Hey, I can see its tiny tonsils wiggling," said Kenny.

It was the worst noise I ever heard. Worse than Dad's car alarm. If our baby cries like that, forget silver curtains. I'm having my room soundproofed!

"Can babies BURST?" I asked anxiously.

Rosie didn't know what to do. She just stood there flapping her hands. Which looks dead weird when you're wearing goggles, orange Marigolds and a bright pink clothes peg!

"I dode thig Borgan liges be," she wailed.

Meanwhile, totally trustworthy Tiffany was still on the phone. We could hear her between screams. I know love makes you blind. But I didn't know it made you deaf as well. Boy, is the Sleepover Club ever out of its depth this time, I thought.

Then suddenly Fliss gave a tiny cough. "I think Morgan's a bit scared of your goggles, Rosie," she said shyly. "Shall I change her?"

Are you amazed? WE were! I don't know why she waited so long, mind you. It's not like the rest of us were falling over ourselves for the honour, or anything! But Fliss really had the magic touch. The minute she unfastened its little sleepsuit, the baby went all quiet and trusting.

I'll spare you the gruesome details. Except to say we had scientific PROOF that Morgan Quormby is a girl baby. (I couldn't tell till then. Probably you couldn't either?) And finally the baby was burbling happily in her cot again. Major relief!

"Fliss, you're a star!" I said. I was ashamed, to tell you the truth. We're always having a go at Fliss for being such an airhead. But when it came to it, she was the only one who didn't freak out!

"I didn't mind," Fliss said, going as pink as Rosie's clothes peg. "I've helped Maria with Posy, loads of times." (Did you remember that Maria is Fliss's dad's girlfriend and Posy is their new baby? You did? Excellent!)

But Rosie was working herself into a major razz. Suddenly she grabbed the phone and screamed down the line, "Tiff! It's not fair. You're supposed to be babysitting. Not us!"

"In a MINUTE!" Tiff screamed back. "This is IMPORTANT, OK! This is my FUTURE!"

Rosie slammed the phone back down. "I can't believe my sister!"

"And she never made our popcorn," I said nastily.

Fliss gave a cheeky little grin. "Never mind," she said. "Spud's cake smells amazing. And all of a sudden I feel dead hungry, don't you?"

I don't know what's come over Fliss! She used to be the Sleepover Club goody-goody.

"Is she thinking what I think she's thinking?" I asked the others.

"WICKED!" we all yelled and charged into the kitchen. Rosie flung open the larder door and there was Tiffany's cake.

"Wow!" said everyone.

It was an awesome triple-layer chocolate sponge, stuffed with whipped cream and smothered with gooey icing. Piped across it were the words: TO SPUD – FOREVER LOVE.

"If Spud eats all that, he'll be really ill," said Fliss primly.

"Boys don't appreciate cake," I said. "It's a known fact."

"And that cake deserves appreciating," sighed Kenny.

"Hmm," said Rosie. "Would it help if someone cut it into slices?"

We only meant to sample it, honestly. But Rosie must have been really mad with her sister, because she carved us these huge slices.

"Are you sure we should have all this?" I asked nervously.

Finally Fliss took the knife off her. "Stop it Rosie. There won't be any left for Spud."

"I don't care," said Rosie sulkily. "Tiff shouldn't be so mean."

None of us really knew what to do. But we couldn't glue the cake back together, could we? So we took our plates into the living room and totally stuffed our faces.

"This cake is to die for, Rosie," Lyndz mumbled.

"We might have to," I pointed out.

Of course Fliss said she could only manage half hers. Even though nicking Spud's cake was her idea! Fliss has this stoopid thing about dieting. We're always on at her about it.

Anyway, by this time, Morgan was whingeing again. "Maybe she's bored," said Fliss. So we took her out of her cot and played with her. First we did 'This little piggy', which Morgan thought was totally ace. Then we got her toys out and she played with those for a bit. Then Kenny decided we should teach

Morgan some Sleepover Club words.

We spent ages getting her to say "Cool". First she giggled like anything. Then she got really fed up. So we bounced her on our knees and sang nursery rhymes. That kept her happy. Well, for a bit. That's the trouble with babies. Nothing works for long. In no time Morgan was grizzling again.

"You're the baby expert, Fliss. What's wrong now?" I asked grumpily.

"She's probably thirsty," said Fliss.

I was cheesed off with Fliss being such a know-all, so I said I'd give Morgan her bottle. You should have seen her sucking away. Just like the baby in *The Simpsons*! I'll be a BRILLIANT sister, I thought. No problemo. Seré una hermana estupenda. But when the juice was gone, Morgan just whinged harder than ever. Babies are SUCH hard work, it's unbelievable! And suddenly I felt totally stressed out. I mean, when our baby was born, how were my parents going to find any time for ME?!

CHAPTER SEVEN

Here's a riddle. How can one small baby make five big girls run round in circles? No, I don't know the answer either. But it's true!

Then I had a brainwave! "Morgan's hungry," I said. "Bet you anything." Heh heh heh. One–nil to me. I beat know-all Fliss that time.

"What do babies eat?" asked Kenny.

"Rusks and things," said Fliss, looking vague.

"Bananas," said Lyndz. "And my baby brother is crazy about fish fingers."

Rosie rushed off. A few minutes later she came back with some mashed-up banana, and toast and jam cut into soldiers. Morgan's face lit up and she made sweet little yummy-yummy noises. Mind you, she didn't exactly eat the food. More squodged it, then crammed fistfuls of goo into her mouth. A lot of it went in her hair!

"Gross," shuddered Kenny.

All at once Morgan stretched out her sticky hands longingly towards Fliss's left-over cake and did her yummy-yummy song.

"Do you want some yummy choccy cake?" I asked.

Do you know what Morgan did next? She opened her mouth like a baby bird and shouted: "GAKE!"

She'd only been with the Sleepover Club for an hour and a half and she'd learned her first word! Well, we had to give her some, didn't we? After she'd been so clever.

Then we heard Tiffany on the move upstairs. I suppose she had to come off the phone some time, but it still gave us a jolt.

"Uh-oh," said Kenny. "Run for it!"

"Rosie!" Tiff yelled down. "Spud's coming

63

round to see his cake in a few minutes. I'm just going to get ready, OK. Then I'll make the popcorn for you."

Are you wondering why her Royal Prissiness was being so matey suddenly? My guess is, now she'd sorted out her love life, she felt bad about making us do her babysitting for her. Unfortunately she was a teensy bit too late.

We looked guiltily at the remains of Spud's cake.

"I'm dead," Rosie gulped. "Totally, totally dead."

"Is Morgan OK?" Tiff called. "I heard her crying."

Morgan beamed happily, dribbling chocolate everywhere. Her sleepsuit was splattered with fruit juice, chocolate cake, jam and mashed banana. She looked like those modern paintings Dad goes bonkers over.

"Morgan's fine," called Rosie feebly. "She just wanted her juice."

"Take as long as you like, Tiff," Kenny yelled.

We heard Tiff run the shower. Rosie threw herself on the sofa. "I'm going to be in doom for ever when Tiff finds out," she wailed.

Fliss mopped up Morgan's face and hands with the baby wipes. She looked a lot cleaner but it put her in a terrible mood.

"Maybe we should sing to her. Posy lurves being sung to," said Fliss.

But we were too shattered, so Lyndz suggested the radio. We fiddled with the stereo till we found a local music station.

"Hey, they're playing *Forever Love*," said Kenny.

Honestly, Morgan is such a cool baby. She started singing along with Juice. "Ooh-ooh-ooh." Cute or what? Then the DJ came on. And guess who was in the studio, wittering about how tough it is being famous? It was Juice himself! The station was running some competition. If you were the first person to phone in with the answer to Juice's question, he popped along to your house and you had to make him a cup of tea. Runners up got Juice CDs and a cap with his autograph on it.

"Great big hairy deal," said Kenny.

"Who'd want Juice to come to their house anyway?" I said. Then we fell about laughing. "The M&Ms!" we yelled.

Rosie sighed. "If we won those CDs, Tiff would totally forgive me! She lurves Juice."

We stared at her, while the DJ droned on about getting permission to use the phone.

"Rosie, you're brilliant!" I said, hugging her.

"Yeah, that's such a cool idea!" said Kenny.

"It could work," agreed Lyndz.

Rosie's eyes went like saucers. "You don't mean, phone in?"

"Sssh," we hissed at her. "We'll miss Juice's question."

"Stand by your phones," said Juice in his new pop star voice. "Can anyone tell me the name of a famous Leicestershire giant?"

"DANIEL LAMBERT!" we shrieked.

"You stoopid wally," added Kenny.

"That's lemon squeezy," I agreed. Every kid in Leicestershire knows about Daniel Lambert!

"Phone in, Rosie," said Fliss

"But I haven't got permission!" Rosie wailed.

"Oh, per-lease," I said, in disgust. "It's only a total emergency. It's only the phone call which is going to save your LIFE!"

Rosie finally caved in. "All right. But you all heard me ask Tiff first, OK?" Then she whispered, "Tiff, please can I use the phone?"

"I think I heard her say 'yes'," I said.

"Me too," said Kenny.

"Definitely," the others nodded.

Rosie made us go out of the room while she phoned in. We earwigged through the door, killing ourselves laughing.

"I'm shaking," she giggled, when we went back in. "Won't it be brilliant if we get those CDs?"

"We will," said Fliss happily. "I can feel it."

"They're practically ours," I agreed.

We were giving each other high fives when the latest All Saints song came on. Kenny turned up the volume. And that was when I had my really bad idea. Only it seemed like such a cool idea at the time. It started like this.

"Isn't Tiff's dress awesome," sighed Fliss. (Yawn yawn yawn.)

"I'd give anything to be as pretty as she is," said Rosie.

So I said, "You'd look ace in Tiff's dress, Rosie."

Why oh WHY did I do that? I didn't mean to get Rosie into any more trouble. I just hate how she puts herself down. I bet you do too, don't you?

"Yeah, right," said Rosie miserably. "You are kidding."

"Try it on." I said. "See for yourself."

"Tiff will be up there titivating for ages," grinned Kenny.

"All right," said Rosie suddenly. "I will. So there!"

She whipped off her sweater and jeans. Fliss lifted down Tiff's dress and handed it to her, giggling. Rosie slipped it over her head. Then she climbed on to a chair to look in the mirror. The dress was miles too big, but when Rosie saw herself, she beamed with surprise. She looked lovely. Well, except for her woolly socks!

"Take them off, dumbo," giggled Fliss.

I waved a pretend wand. "Beautiful Cinders, you shall go to the ball!"

Then I went a bit crazy. I grabbed Rosie's mum's hat from the hall and danced around in it. Fliss picked Morgan up and danced her round too. Soon everyone was whirling round the room.

Sometimes Rosie has the worst luck. One minute she was dancing happily. Then she caught her foot and went flying. She landed on her bottom. Guess what she landed in?

Fliss's messy, chocolatey plate.

And she'd got chocolate all over Tiff's new dress!

CHAPTER EIGHT

"Take it off, quick!" Fliss told her. "We'll get a cloth."

Rosie scrambled into her jeans. The rest of us rushed the dress into the kitchen and sponged away with Vanish. But the stain didn't. Vanish, I mean.

"It's only on the back," I said, trying to cheer Rosie up.

"Yeah, if you hang it up, she won't notice," said Kenny.

"Take it to the cleaners," said Fliss. "They do a same-day service. You can pick it up before Tiff gets home from the Happy Shopper."

"But how do I GET there?" wailed Rosie.

"We'll figure something out," I promised. But I felt really bad for her.

Fliss gave me the baby and helped Kenny put the dress back. I rocked Morgan absent-mindedly. She snuggled up like a sleepy little bear and started yawning. Hey, I thought. I'm good at this!

"There," said Kenny. "Tiff won't suspect a thing."

The door bell went.

"You let Spud in, Frankie," Rosie pleaded. "He'll see I've been crying."

It seems stoopid now, but I truly didn't twig who was on Rosie's step. I did think Spud looked kind of taller. But I put it down to the weird glass in Rosie's front door. Anyway, I was having trouble with the security chain. Plus Rosie's mum's hat kept sliding over my eyes. But I finally got the door open. And there... was... JUICE!

I gawped long enough to notice he had a

photographer and two massive bodyguards with him. Then I slammed the door in his face in a total panic. We hadn't won the CDs and the baseball cap after all. We'd won Juice!!!

The door bell went again. This time Juice kept his finger there.

"Let him in, you idiots!" shrieked Tiff.

The others came to see what was taking me so long.

"Why did you slam the door on Spud?" Rosie asked, bewildered.

"I didn't," I hissed. "It's Juice."

"Yeah, right," grinned Kenny. "Nice try, Frankie."

"It is! It's him!" squeaked Fliss. "I'm going to faint!"

"But I want those CDs for Tiff," wailed Rosie.

I was hopping from foot to foot. "But what are we going to DO?"

"Make him his stupid cup of tea," suggested Kenny. "Then he'll go away."

I opened the door again, faking a smile. "Hiya. So we won! Wow!"

"Hiya, everyone," said Rosie feebly. "Come in."

"Frankie didn't mean to shut the door earlier. She was just overwhelmed," Kenny explained. "She's never met a pop singer before."

Juice gave a lazy smile. "That's OK. It's a kind of weird situation."

Oops! Hang on a tick. I'm putting this story on hold, so I can give you vital background info.

The truth is, I was seriously churned up at this point. You guessed Kenny was fibbing her face off to get me out of a sticky situation, didn't you? Excellent! I think I told you before, that I used to know Juice, in his Julian Whately life? Now there's no way he'd ever remember me, OK?

But unfortunately, *his* mum told *my* mum all kinds of highly embarrassing stories about him. Stories I'm sure Juice would much rather not remember.

You see, in his Julian days Juice was not remotely cool. In fact, he was so incredibly

73

sad and weedy, he was constantly being bullied at school. And one day, after gym, some really stoo-pid boys deliberately stole his trousers.

Can you believe that poor old Julian/Juice had to walk down the school corridor to the secretary's office in this absolutely *ancient* pair of Flintstone boxer shorts, with all the other kids laughing themselves sick?

Now, I'm not very proud of this, OK, but one day Juice's name came up in conversation, and I found myself splurting out this tasty bit of goss to everyone. Then I totally forgot about it till now.

So when Juice turned up on Rosie's doorstep, I was just about going into orbit, in case the others cracked up laughing right in front of him.

But they didn't. And I didn't. And you wouldn't have either!

Because believe me, when you see Juice in person, you wouldn't connect him in a million years with that picked-on kid in tatty Flintstone undies.

Why? Because he's an absolute BABE!

I mean, obviously Juice has been hitting the spinach lately, because he's got actual muscles now. But more than that, he's just totally cool and laid back and, well, definitely CUTE!!!

We were all so gobsmacked, we stood around like waxworks, not knowing what to do next. Finally Rosie said, "Do I make just Juice a cup of tea, or shall I make some for everyone?"

"Don't mind if I do," said one of the bodyguards chirpily.

"Two sugars, thanks," said the other one.

"Diet Coke," said Juice. "No ice."

We took him into the living room and Juice threw himself on the sofa. "Nice baby," he said. "My sister's got a kid about the same age."

"Which of you little girls is the lucky winner?" asked the photographer.

Don't you absolutely HATE it when grown-ups treat you as if you've only got half a brain cell? So does Kenny.

"All of us won," she scowled.

"Yeah," said Lyndz. "The entire Sleepover Club."

Juice then made us tell him about our club. He was really interested. We were just explaining what you do at sleepovers when Rosie came back with the drinks.

Morgan was moaning again. It's probably not too easy to get to sleep, with the whole Sleepover Club, a pop singer, one photographer and two bodyguards in your room. Plus there was something else bothering her, but we didn't find that out till later.

"Is the little baby sleeping over too?" asked the photographer, in his 'let's humour the kiddies' tone.

Kenny rolled her eyes. "As if."

Juice swung Morgan up on to his knee. He looked a bit amazed when he clocked her modern-art sleepsuit. "Man, you should audition for Persil," he told her.

We giggled. And I don't know how it happened, but somehow we ended up telling Juice about Spud's cake and how we'd wanted the CDs for Tiff.

Juice wasn't a bit offended. He fell about laughing. "I'd better get those CDs to your sister, FAST."

"That would be brilliant!" Rosie's face lit up.

"Can we just have that photograph, everyone?" asked the photographer. I think he felt quite left out. He made us squeeze on to the sofa with Juice and do cheesy smiles. But his flashbulb wouldn't work.

So Fliss told Juice about Morgan singing along to *Forever Love*. "Will you sing it for us now?" she asked, going bright red.

The rest of us were dead embarrassed. But Juice just started singing, right there on Rosie's sofa. It was so-o-o sweet. Morgan gazed at him with total adoration. So did Fliss. (Surprise, surprise!)

I think that's when the photographer snapped the picture. But I didn't actually notice a flash. You see, I'd seen a funny expression flicker across Morgan's face. And I was just going to tell Juice to stop jiggling her about, but before I got the chance, she gave a worried little cry. Then she did it.

Morgan sicked up her fruit juice, mashed banana, toast, jam and stolen chocolate cake all over her and Juice.

Juice jumped to his feet, totally shocked. His bodyguards had already dived out of the way. (Bodyguards have excellent reflexes.)

Then Morgan gave a lopsided grin. I suppose she was feeling heaps better now. And in a clear little voice, she said, "Cool."

It didn't really seem like the right moment to tell Morgan how clever she was.

"Will you take her, Frankie?" said Juice politely. "I'd better get some clean clothes. We're doing a gig at some university tonight."

I know it's really wimpy, but I'm not wild about touching people with sick on them. "Fliss?" I said hopefully.

"Ask Kenny," said Fliss. "I did the nappy."

"No way," growled Kenny.

"Lyndz?"

Lyndz shook her head. "Uh-uh."

Things weren't looking too bright. Then who do you think came dashing downstairs, all pretty and glowing from her shower?

You've got to hand it to Tiffany Cartwright. Give her a real crisis – sisters fainting in the supermarket, or unexpectedly finding her favourite pop singer covered in baby sick – and she's a total star.

She didn't let herself down by staring at Juice adoringly. She didn't squeak or squeal. She didn't even, like, *glance* in the mirror to check her hair looked OK.

There was just a split second when she froze halfway down the stairs. But it was just a *weensy* split second. And we were the only ones who noticed.

Tiff whisked Morgan out of Juice's arms. "Perhaps you'd like to use our bathroom to freshen up, Juice," she said, as if she talked to pop stars every day. "Upstairs, second on the left. Towels in the airing cupboard."

"Thanks," said Juice bravely. His bodyguards bounded after him. I think they were quite scared of Tiff.

"I'll see myself out, girls," said the photographer.

Then came the moment we were dreading.

"As for you," Tiff said, giving us the evil eye as she carefully peeled Morgan's sleepsuit off, "you've got some serious explaining to do."

CHAPTER NINE

Luckily, the baby went into a major screaming fit. Tiffany paced the room, patting Morgan's back, looking stressed out. Like she was the one who'd been babysitting all night!!

Juice and his bodyguards thundered back downstairs. Poor Juice. His clothes were ruined.

"Later, girls, yeah?" he said, climbing into his awesome car, and they zoomed away down Rosie's street.

Tiff took Morgan upstairs and for a few

minutes the baby's howls were muffled by the sound of running water.

"It's not fair," said Rosie miserably. "Why did Morgan have to throw up? Juice will never send Tiff those CDs now. I'm in so-o much trouble. Tiff's mad NOW, and she doesn't know about her dress yet."

"Or about Spud's cake," Lyndz pointed out.

"Thanks for reminding us," said Kenny.

The door bell went again. It really was Spud this time. But before he could get in the door, Tiff came downstairs, out of breath and sopping wet, with a screaming baby under her arm. You'd think she'd been on the giant flume at Alton Towers, not bathing some little kid!

One problem with Spud is he's not big on timing. "Hiya Tiff," he beamed. "Where's my cake? I'm starving."

"Not now Spud," said Tiff fiercely. "I've got my hands full!" And she shut the door in his face. After all we'd gone through for her! We were in total shock!!

Tiffany dressed Morgan in her clean sleepsuit. I think Morgan knew Tiff was in a bad mood. She threw herself around, bellowing at the top of her lungs.

"What a nightmare," groaned Tiff. "The Quormbys will be back soon. I thought Morgan was supposed to sleep through the night."

I held out my arms. "Shall I take her?" I said.

Looking a bit doubtful, Tiff handed Morgan over. And guess what! Morgan snuggled up like a kitten and fell fast asleep. Don't tell the others, but I think I'm a totally magic babysitter, don't you?

But Tiff was looking panicky. "Quick, put her in her cot. Someone's coming." She was practically wetting herself! But the footsteps went on past.

I tucked Morgan into her cot. "Night night," I said. "Mind the bugs don't bite." We tiptoed out.

"Have you girls any idea what Morgan's been eating?" said Tiff. "Some of those stains looked just like chocolate."

We all stared at the floor. But instead of having a go at us, Tiff said, "You girls had better go to bed before Mum gets back. I'll tidy up down here."

"Heh heh heh! We're off the hook, my hearties," hissed Kenny. We charged upstairs. Almost made it too.

Then Tiff called, "Rosie, what was Juice doing here?"

"Uh-oh," whispered Lyndz.

"Oh," said Rosie. She gulped. "That was just a mistake."

"A famous pop singer came to our house, by mistake?"

"We sort of won him. In a radio phone-in," said poor Rosie. "We were trying to win the CDs. For you."

"Why?" said Tiff suspiciously.

It's weird. Rosie Cartwright can hold out on her friends for hours. But when it comes to her family, Rosie's what my gran calls "an open book". Rosie took a really big breath. Uh-oh, I thought.

"If you want to know, we ate most of Spud's cake," she yelled. "I was mad with you for making us do your babysitting, OK!"

Then Rosie marched into her room. We went in after her. But we didn't know what to say, so we started getting ready for bed.

A few minutes later, we heard footsteps coming up the path. A key turned in the lock.

"No, she was a little angel," we heard Tiff say brightly. "But she dribbled some of her juice on her sleepsuit, so I put it in the wash." Then we couldn't hear any more.

"Oooh, liar liar! Tiffany's pants are on fire," giggled Lyndz.

"Sssh. Rosie's mum will be up in a minute," I hissed.

We scrambled into our night things. I don't know if you remember, but Rosie's the only girl in the Sleepover Club who's got her own double bed. Cool or what! The first time we slept over, we all piled in, but it was too much of a squash! Now we toss for it, to see who sleeps on the floor. It was Kenny and Lyndz. Yippee!

We dived into our sleeping bags, seconds before Rosie's mum opened the door. "Having fun, everyone?" she asked.

"Yes!" we chorused. She put out the light and closed the door. We heard her go back downstairs. This is our favourite sleepover moment, when we switch on our torches and have our feast. Well, four of us switched our torches on. But Rosie stayed where she was with the covers over her head. She'd been really quiet since she yelled at Tiff. Then the bed started shaking with sobs. I patted her shoulder.

"Don't cry, Rosie," I said.

Rosie rolled over and switched on her torch. "I'm not, you moron. I'm laughing!"

I felt such an idiot!

"Just wait," Rosie shrieked, "till we tell the M&Ms that Juice came to our sleepover!"

Kenny cracked up. "They'll chew the carpet!"

"Froth at the mouth," spluttered Fliss.

"Spit nails," I giggled.

Lyndz hugged herself. "They'll NEVER forgive us."

"They'll NEVER believe us either," I pointed out.

"Who cares! It's definitely one–nil to the Sleepover Club," Lyndz said.

Kenny punched the air. "One nil! More like FIVE!"

"Sssh! I'm writing in my diary," said Fliss. She scribbled away, while we finished up the bubble stuff in the sword. Bubbles look incredibly spooky by torchlight.

"Want to hear?" Fliss said at last. She started reading aloud. "It's been the most hectic sleepover ever. We had to babysit for a cool baby called Morgan. My best thing was when Juice came to Rosie's house and sang *Forever Love*. My worst was when Rosie sat in my plate and got chocolate on Tiff's dress."

Then Fliss looked up and gave a little gasp.

Tiffany had come in very softly, so no one noticed. She didn't yell at us though. She just dumped a bowl of popcorn in the middle of Rosie's floor.

"Enjoy," she said. We stared at her nervously.

Kenny sniffed the bowl like a tracker dog. "It's not poisoned, is it?"

Tiff laughed. "Brownie's honour!"

"But I spoilt your dress!" cried Rosie.

"Thanks, but I'd figured that out for myself," said Tiff calmly. "It's OK. I'll take it to the dry cleaners on Monday."

Tiff was being so nice to us, I felt terrible. I'd have gone ballistic if it was my dress, wouldn't you?

"We'll chip in," I said. "Rosie didn't want to try it on, you know. We made her."

Tiff took a deep breath. "Look, I don't blame you for wanting to pay me back. I was totally out of order," she said. "You could have dropped me in it. But you didn't. Let's call it quits."

"All RIGHT!" we said, at exactly the same moment. Then we said, "Jinx!" and fell about laughing.

Tiff closed the door while we were still giggling.

"Let's have our feast, before I fall asleep," yawned Kenny.

As well as the popcorn, we had snowballs, rainbow drops, Pringles and those licorice wands with fizzy sherbet inside them. You wouldn't believe how hungry you get babysitting!

"We earned this," said Lyndz, through her mouthful of snowball.

"Yeah," I said. "All's well that ends well."

But it wasn't over. Nothing like...

CHAPTER TEN

Slow down a bit! We're almost there, and I've got a question for you! How come Juice is so good-looking now he's famous?!!

I think that's one reason why Tiff let us off the hook. She thought it was really cool meeting Juice. Spud was dead jealous when he found out. He won't forget their anniversary again in a hurry!

Here's Rosie's house, look. The really big one. Quick, duck down! They're in Rosie's front room waiting for me. Lucky Mr Quormby's got his back to the window.

I'm not wimping out. No way! I just thought you'd like to hear the end of the story. I'll tell you the good news first, OK? The stain totally came out of Tiffany's dress, so she wore it to the dance after all.

Shall I tell you the bad news now? It's bad all right. Bad as can be.

Remember that photographer who came to Rosie's house? You thought that cheesy picture was just for Juice's private album, didn't you? Wrong, wrong, WRONG!

The Quormbys had a big shock when they saw their precious baby girl plastered all over the front page of the Mercury. They thought she'd been asleep in her cot, not grooving the night away with pop stars!

It was an excellent picture. You could see everything. The pattern on Rosie's mum's sofa. The soppy smile on Fliss's face as Juice sang to us. The photograph was so sharp, you could even see the modern art splatters on Morgan's sleepsuit. And to think we nearly got away with it...

I don't blame the Quormbys for being livid

with us. But now the M&Ms are convinced we invited Juice to our sleepover just to spite them. I hate to think what they're cooking up to pay us back. (Though I'd lurve to have seen their faces when they saw that picture in the Mercury. Heh heh heh!)

So, like I told you, I'm lying low, until the fuss dies down. It'll be good practice for when I'm a world-famous actress, dodging the press! But before I go, let me tell you something I found out at Rosie's sleepover. Two things actually.

1) I am going to make an excellent big sister

and...

2) I'd better catch up on my sleep while I can!!

OK, I'm going in to face the music now. Cross your fingers and thumbs, won't you. It's been great seeing you. Bye!!

and for Dec '99,
a MILLENNIUM SPECIAL →

Happy New Year, Sleepover Club!

It's party time! The Millennium is looming, and the girls plan a mega-special New Year sleepover. But what with Frankie's mum due to have her baby at any moment, and Fliss's mum with her Big Secret, nothing's going to end up going to plan. So what else is new...!!

Pop on your party hat and drop in on the fun!

P.T.O. for a sneak preview →

CHAPTER ONE

Hi there. I know what you're going to say. "Frankie, you're late!"

I'm right aren't I? That's what the others are always saying these days. It always used to be Lyndz who was late, and I was super-dooper organised. Not any more! My house is so manic at the moment it's a wonder I ever get out at all. But I'll tell you all about that in a minute. We really ought to sit down and catch up on all the goss. Fliss is still recovering. Poor Fliss, it all got a bit much for her – and her mum. But Kenny was in seventh heaven because she managed to do her doctor bit at last. And Lyndz and Rosie, well they're still hiccuping and giggling about it whenever anyone even mentions what happened.

☆

Sorry I'm gabbling, but there's just so much to tell you. Come on, let's sit over here and I'll fill you in on all the details. But boy, where do I start? OK, well I guess the beginning's as good a place as any.

It all started before Christmas. No, much sooner than that. It all really started months ago when I found out that Mum was pregnant. I'd wanted a little baby brother or sister for as long as I could remember, and when I found out that Mum was expecting one I was totally blown away by the excitement. The others all tried their hardest to put me off by giving me loads of grisly details.

"Babies are just totally embarrassing," warned Lyndz. "Didn't you learn anything when we were helping Rosie's sister with her babysitting last time? Babies are either pooing or being sick. And my older brothers aren't much better."

Poor Lyndz has four brothers and she reckons that they make her life a misery.

"At least you'll be a lot older than your brother or sister," reasoned Kenny. "You'll be able to boss it about all the time. How cool is that!"

Her eyes gleamed at the thought. Molly the Monster, as you know, is only a year older than Kenny, but is one major super-witch when it comes to being horrible.

"Yeah, when you're wanting to go out, it'll be pestering you to play!" laughed Rosie. "Tiff always says that I'm a major pain when she's getting glammed up, and she's only four years older than me! But I'm sure that you'll have a lot more patience than her," she added. "And you won't have a boyfriend as ugly as Spud either."

The others all nodded.

"I won't have a boyfriend at all!" I said indignantly.

"Yes you will!" snorted Fliss. "When the baby is our age, you'll be twenty! Imagine that. You'll probably be at university then. You might even be married!"

We all guffawed.

"No way!" I yelled. "You'll be married to Ryan Scott, more like!"

☆

Fliss just blushed and went all giggly – as usual!

We had loads of conversations like that, and the others always told me horror stories about being a sister. Now don't get me wrong. I was still desperate to have a baby to look after, but the more they told me, the more nervous I got. I mean, it just seemed so long since I'd found out about the baby, and it wasn't even due until January.

"I wish it would hurry up!" I told Mum one day at the beginning of December. "I just want to get on with being a big sister."

"Well, I'm not ready to be a new mum again just yet, thank you very much!" she laughed. "We've still got far too much to do!"

That was true. They still hadn't sorted out where the baby was going to sleep for one thing. At this rate, it would be sharing Pepsi's basket in the kitchen!

"But how will I know if I'll be any good as a sister?" I asked Mum.

"You'll be just great!" she smiled, ruffling my hair. "If you're so worried, you could always

☆

practise on something. There are some schools which make students look after a bag of flour as though it's a baby. I know it sounds weird, but it gets them used to having someone else to think about."

"You want me to push a bag of flour about in a pram?" I asked, open-mouthed.

"It doesn't have to be a bag of flour," Mum explained. "You could use one of your old dolls. The important thing is to treat it as though it really is a baby. No dumping it under your bed when you're fed up with it. Just look after it for a day or so and I guarantee it will open your eyes."

Yes, I know, I know – it sounds really wacky, doesn't it? But I thought it might be worth a try. I went up to my room and pulled the box of old dolls out of my cupboard. I hadn't looked at them for absolutely ages and it felt really weird holding them again.

"You're way too old for all this, Frankie," I told myself.

But I got them all out anyway and sat them in a line on my bed. I felt kind of funny seeing

☆

them like that, because it brought back memories of when I was little. I had this one doll I used to call Diz which I used to take everywhere with me. I picked it up now, and it looked so tiny and shabby. I felt really bad, like I'd abandoned it or something. But I couldn't use that as my baby because it just didn't look right. It was too small for a start and had matted wool hair. The others didn't look much better, to be honest with you.

Then I spotted 'the doll with no name'. A friend of Mum's had given it to me just as I was growing out of my doll phase and I'd never really played with it. But it was about the right size for a baby. It had no hair and it still smelt kind of clean and new.

"Come on then!" I said, picking her up. "You can be my baby. Are you going to be a good girl?" I cooed, tickling her under the chin.

I was amazed how quickly I got into all the baby stuff. Before long it didn't seem weird at all to be wandering round with a doll. But you know my friends. As soon as they saw me with

☆

the doll one Saturday, they thought I'd lost it completely.

"Francesca Thomas, have you gone mad?" screeched Kenny when she saw me carrying Izzy. (I called my doll Isobel, Izzy for short, because that's what I wanted Mum to call the baby if she had a girl.)

"I'm just winding her after her feed!" I explained, patting Izzy's back.

"I'll wind you in a minute!" she yelled. "What are you like?"

No amount of explaining what I was doing would make her shut up. And the others weren't much better. Even Fliss had a go at me.

"You look really silly, Frankie," she hissed. "I wish you'd put that stupid doll down. It's going to be really embarrassing if anyone sees us."

I must admit that I did feel a bit of a dipstick taking it to the shops with us, but a deal is a deal. Mum said that I had to treat the doll just like a real baby. If I had to go to the shops then it would just have to come with me. I couldn't leave Izzy at home, could I?

☆

"Couldn't you ask your mum to babysit?" asked Lyndz. Kenny rolled her eyes.

"I don't think so. I'm supposed to be learning how to be a big sister," I explained. "Mum already knows how to be a mum, so asking her to babysit a doll would be a bit pointless."

"The whole thing's pointless if you ask me," grumbled Kenny. "Well, are we going to the shops or not?"

To start with, I made a sort of sling with my scarf and kept Izzy snuggled under my jacket. The December wind was pretty fierce and I didn't want her to get cold.

"You are sad, sad, sad," chanted Kenny, as I kept fussing beneath my jacket.

"At least no one can see the doll," said Fliss. "You just look fat!"

"Thanks very much!" I said, feeling a bit miffed.

But it soon got uncomfortable having Izzy in one position so I started wriggling and jiggling, trying to move her about. It didn't help that her arms and legs weren't all

☆

squidgy like a real baby's. They were rigid plastic and kept digging into me.

"Don't do that, Frankie!" Rosie reprimanded me. "You look as though you've got ants in your pants or something. People are looking at you."

It was true. There were hundreds of people about doing their Christmas shopping, and I could sense that most of them were glancing at me and frowning.

"Maybe I should just show them Izzy," I suggested, unzipping my jacket.

"Don't do that!" the others all yelled together.

"That would be a major embarrassment for all of us," hissed Kenny.

"Hey, what's that poster?" Fliss suddenly shouted at the top of her voice. She was being so OTT, it was obvious that she was trying to divert our attention. She sort of galloped over to the noticeboard at the end of the high street. The rest of us cracked up and galloped after her. It wasn't easy with a doll poking you in the chest with every step, I can tell you.

☆

"It's advertising a Millennium New Year's Eve party at the church hall," explained Fliss, standing in front of the poster. "Do you think we'll be able to go?"

"Not a chance," said Rosie. "My mum's only ever let me stay up to see the New Year in once, and that was because I was sick."

"I'm not sure I'd want to go anyway," Kenny said. "It'll be full of boring old duffers who we don't even know. It'd be much better to have a New Year's Eve party of our own."

"Yes!" we all screamed. "Why don't we? It'd be so cool!"

"We should try to organise a special New Year's Eve sleepover," I suggested. "I mean, we're usually awake till well past midnight when we're together anyway. It would be great to stay up properly. Everyone else'll be up too, because of the year 2000, so who could object?"

We were so excited we started doing a little dance together on the pavement. And that's when Izzy fell out of my jacket and bounced on to the ground.

☆

"Oh no!" I screamed, picking her up. "I've killed her!"

"Erm, earth to Frankie!" hooted Kenny. "It is only a doll, you know!"

"But it's supposed to be my baby sister," I spluttered. "What if I do that to her?"

"Don't be crazy!" shrieked Lyndz. "Do you think your parents would really let us loose in charge of their baby? I don't think so!"

"But even so," I wailed. "I was supposed to take care of Izzy and I haven't. I'm going to be a useless sister!"

Fliss led me over to a nearby bench and we all sat down.

"You're going to be a great sister, Frankie," she reassured me. "That was just an accident when you forgot about the d... I mean, Izzy."

"But what if I forget about the real baby when I'm supposed to be looking after it?" I asked.

"Believe me, you never forget when you've got a baby around," Lyndz grinned. "They never stop crying. And they usually smell disgusting too!"

☆

I was rocking Izzy in my arms and the others were all bending over her, just like she was real.

"Well I've seen everything now!" boomed a loud voice.

We looked up quickly, but with sinking hearts we already knew who it was. Why had the M&Ms picked that exact minute to walk past us?

"Aw, has Francesca got a baby? Diddums," said Emma Hughes in a stupid voice.

"Does she like playing with her dolly then?" cooed Emma's sidekick Emily Berryman.

"I always knew you were a big baby, Thomas!" cackled Emma. "I grew out of dolls when I was about four. You lot have never grown up, have you?"

Kenny was seething, I could sense it.

"Frankie's taking part in some scientific research, if you must know," she said in her weariest voice. "Not that you'd understand."

"Oh right, that's the first time I've heard playing with dolls called 'scientific research',"

☆

sneered Emily. "Why don't you face it? You're a load of little kids!"

They both screamed with laughter and tottered down the high street on their platform wedges.

"I don't believe that!" Fliss had her head in her hands. "Of all the people to see us with that stupid doll!"

"They'll never let us forget it," moaned Rosie. "It'll be all round the school on Monday!"

"Not if I've got anything to do with it," fumed Kenny through gritted teeth.

And when Kenny spoke like that the rest of us knew that it meant trouble. Trouble with a capital T!

To be continued...

Sleepover Girls Go Snowboarding

Kenny's getting starry-eyed about her new mate Nick, a snowboarding whizz who works at the sports shop. Nothing less than a trip to the local snowboarding centre is called for! But is Nick all he's cracked up to be...?

Pack up your sleepover kit and head for the slopes!

25

Sleepover Club 2000

It's a new year, a new century and a new leaf for the Sleepover Club, as Cuddington Primary School hatches its very own Millennium project. The gang have to come up with some bright ideas, and fast! But no one bargains on Fliss's mum coming up with the craziest idea of all...

Pack up your sleepover kit and head for the FUTURE!

Order Form

To order direct from the publishers, just make a list of the titles you want and fill in the form below:

Name ....

Address ....

....

....

Send to: Dept 6, HarperCollins Publishers Ltd, Westerhill Road, Bishopbriggs, Glasgow G64 2QT.

Please enclose a cheque or postal order to the value of the cover price, plus:

UK & BFPO: Add £1.00 for the first book, and 25p per copy for each additional book ordered.

Overseas and Eire: Add £2.95 service charge. Books will be sent by surface mail but quotes for airmail despatch will be given on request.

A 24-hour telephone ordering service is available to holders of Visa, MasterCard, Amex or Switch cards on 0141- 772 2281.

Collins
An *Imprint* of HarperCollins*Publishers*